金子みすゞ 心の詩集
The Poetry of Misuzu

よしだみどり 編［英訳・絵］

特別付録CD［歌・朗読］

藤原書店

金子みすゞ　心の詩集

もくじ

The Poetry of Misuzu
― CONTENTS ―

星とたんぽぽ	6
わらい	8
こだまでしょうか	10
私と小鳥と鈴と	12
お日さん、雨さん	14
不思議	16
犬	18
女の子	20
こおろぎ	22
睫毛の虹	24
お菓子	26
みんなを好きに	28
あるとき	30
こころ	32

◇◇◇◇◇◇◇◇◇◇◇◇◇◇◇◇◇◇◇◇◇◇◇◇◇◇◇◇◇◇

Stars and a Dandelion	7
A Laughter	8
Is It an Echo ?	11
A Bell, a Little Bird, and Me	13
The Sun, The Rain	14
Mystery	17
The Dog	19
Girls	21
A Cricket	23
Rainbows on Eyelashes	25
Sweets	27
I want to learn to like Everybody and Everything	29
Once	31
Hearts	33

口真似（くちまね）	34
さびしいとき	36
闇夜の星（やみよのほし）	38
葉（は）っぱの赤ちゃん	40
お花だったら	42
木	44
花のたましい	46
蓮（はす）と鶏（にわとり）	48
蜂（はち）と神（かみ）さま	50
繭（まゆ）と墓（はか）	52
明（あか）るい方（ほう）へ	54
土（つち）	56
草原（そうげん）	58
露（つゆ）	60

◇◇◇◇◇◇◇◇◇◇◇◇◇◇◇◇◇◇◇◇◇◇◇◇◇◇

Mimic	35
When I'm Lonely	37
A Star in the Dark	39
Tiny Baby Leaves	41
If I Were a Flower	43
A Tree	45
A Flower's Soul	47
Lotus and Hens	48
God and a Bee	51
Cocoons and Graves	53
Towards the Light	55
The Ground	57
Grass	58
The Dewdrop	61

あとがき　84

帆(ほ)　80

お魚(さかな)　78

大漁(たいりょう)　76

硝子(がらす)のなか　74

積(つ)もった雪(ゆき)　72

祇園社(ぎおんしゃ)　70

八百屋(やおや)のお鳩(はと)　68

極楽寺(ごくらくじ)　66

ふうせん　64

ばあやのお話(はなし)　62

Nanny's Story　63
A Balloon　65
Gokurakuji Temple　67
The Doves at the Green Grocer's　69
Gion Shrine　71
A Pile of Snow　72
Through the Glass　75
A Big Catch　77
Fish　79
Sails　81

Postscript　85

金子みすゞ　心の詩集

The Poetry of Misuzu

星とたんぽぽ

青いお空の底ふかく、
海の小石のそのように、
夜がくるまで沈んでる、
昼のお星は眼にみえぬ。
　見えぬけれどもあるんだよ、
　見えぬものでもあるんだよ。

散ってすがれたたんぽぽの、
瓦のすきに、だァまって、
春のくるまでかくれてる、
つよいその根は眼にみえぬ。

見えぬけれどもあるんだよ、
見えぬものでもあるんだよ。

Stars and a Dandelion

In the deep blue sky,
Like the pebbles at the bottom of the sea,
The daytime stars, sinking until night comes,
Are invisible to our eyes.
   But though we can't see them, they are there,
   Things invisible are still there.

A Fallen withered dandelion,
Silently hides in the cracks of a roof tile,
Its strong roots, waiting until spring comes,
Are invisible to our eyes.
   But though we can't see them, they are there,
   Things invisible are still there.

わらい

それはきれいな薔薇いろで、
芥子つぶよりかちいさくて、
こぼれて土に落ちたとき、
ぱっと花火がはじけるように、
おおきな花がひらくのよ。

もしも泪がこぼれるように、
こんな笑いがこぼれたら、
どんなに、どんなに、
きれいでしょう。

A Laughter

It's a pretty rosy color,
　Smaller than a poppy seed,
When it drops to the ground,
　A big flower blooms,
As when a firework would pop out.

If you would laugh like the popping flower,
　As when a tear would drop down,
How pretty, how wonderful,
　It would be.

こだまでしょうか

「遊ぼう」っていうと
「遊ぼう」っていう。

「馬鹿」っていうと
「馬鹿」っていう。

「もう遊ばない」っていうと
「遊ばない」っていう。

そうして、あとで
さみしくなって、

Is It an Echo?

When I say "Let's play,"
   It says "Let's play."

When I say "Fool,"
   It says "Fool."

When I say "I'm not going to play with you anymore,"
   It says "I'm not going to play."

And so, later
   I become sad,

Then I say "Sorry,"
   It says "Sorry."

Is it an echo?
   No, it's any one of us.

「ごめんね」っていうと
「ごめんね」っていう。

こだまでしょうか、
いいえ、誰でも。

私と小鳥と鈴と

私が両手をひろげても、
お空はちっとも飛べないが、
飛べる小鳥は私のように、
地面を速くは走れない。

私がからだをゆすっても、
きれいな音は出ないけど、
あの鳴る鈴は私のように
たくさんな唄は知らないよ。

鈴と、小鳥と、それから私、
みんなちがって、みんないい。

A Bell, a Little Bird, and Me

Even though I open my arms wide,
   I still can't fly in the sky at all,
But a little bird who can fly,
   Can't run on the ground as fast as me.

Even though I shake my body,
   I still can't make a sound as beautiful as a bell,
But that ringing bell doesn't know
   As many songs as me.

A bell, a little bird, and me,
   We're all different, and all wonderful.

お日さん、雨さん

ほこりのついた
芝草(しばくさ)を
雨さん洗(あら)って
くれました。

洗ってぬれた
芝草を
お日さんほして
くれました。

こうして私(わたし)が

The Sun, The Rain

The rain washed the dusty grass.
The sun dried the wetty grass.

For me to lie on the grass, like this
And let me look up at the sky, the best.

ねころんで
空をみるのに
よいように。

不思議

私は不思議でたまらない、
黒い雲からふる雨が、
銀にひかっていることが。

私は不思議でたまらない、
青い桑の葉たべている、
蚕が白くなることが。

私は不思議でたまらない、
だれもいじらぬ夕顔が、
ひとりでぱらりと開くのが。

Mystery

I can't stop wondering,
Why raindrops that fall from black clouds,
Are shiny silver.

I can't stop wondering,
Why silkworms eating green mulberry leaves,
Become white.

I can't stop wondering,
How the bottle gourd bursts into bloom all by itself,
Without anybody touching it.

I can't stop wondering,
Why whoever I ask just laughs,
And says, it's no wonder at all.

私は不思議でたまらない、
誰にきいても笑ってて、
あたりまえだ、ということが。

犬

うちのだりあの咲いた日に
酒屋のクロは死にました。
おもてであそぶわたしらを、
いつでも、おこるおばさんが、
おろおろ泣いて居りました。
その日、学校でそのことを
おもしろそうに、話して、
ふっとさみしくなりました。

The Dog

The day my dahlia blossomed
    Kuro, the dog at the 'sake' shop, died.

The lady at the 'sake' shop,
    Who always scolds us for playing outside,
    Was helplessly lost and sobbing.

That day, at school
    While I was making fun of her,

I suddenly felt sad.

                        *sake = Japanese rice wine

Girls

A so-called
Girl,
Should not climb trees
You know.

If she walks on stilts
She's a tomboy,
And if she spins tops
She's a fool.

I know
All this,
Because I've been scolded
For every one of them.

竹馬乗ったら
おてんばで、
打ち独楽するのは
お馬鹿なの。

私はこいだけ
知ってるの、
だって一ぺんずつ
叱られたから。

こおろぎ

こおろぎの
脚が片っぽ
もげました。
追っかけた
たまは叱って
やったけど、
しらじらと
秋の日ざしは
こともなく、

こおろぎの
脚は片っぽ
もげてます。

A Cricket

A cricket
 One of his legs
 Has been broken off.

Of course, I scolded
 Tama the cat
 For chasing him,

The autumn sunlight
 Not knowing anything
 Stayed calm and untroubled,

A cricket
 One of his legs
 Is broken off.

睫毛(まつげ)の虹(にじ)

ふいても、ふいても
湧(わ)いてくる、
涙(なみだ)のなかで
おもうこと。

——あたしはきっと、
もらい児(ご)よ——

まつげのはしの
うつくしい、
虹を見い見い
おもうこと。

Rainbows on Eyelashes

I wipe and wipe,
Yet they keep flowing,
Within my tears
A thought arises.

— I must be
　An adopted child —

While I look and look
At the beautiful rainbows,
On the tips of my eyelashes,
A thought arises.

— I wonder what
　Today's teatime snack will be —

お菓子

いたずらに一つかくした
弟のお菓子。
たべるもんかと思ってて、
たべてしまった、
一つのお菓子。

母さんが二つッていったら、
どうしよう。

おいてみて
とってみてまたおいてみて、
それでも弟が来ないから、

Sweets

Just for fun, I hid
    One of my brother's sweets.
Though I was determined not to eat it,
    I ate it anyway,
    His sweet.

But what would I do if my mother said,
    There were two.

I put it back
    Then took it and put it back again,
But still my brother didn't come,
    So I ate it.
His second sweet.

Bitter sweet.
Sad sweet.

たべてしまった、
二つめのお菓子。
にがいお菓子、
かなしいお菓子。

みんなを好きに

私(わたし)は好きになりたいな、
何(なん)でもかんでもみいんな。

葱(ねぎ)も、トマトも、おさかなも、
残(のこ)らず好きになりたいな。

うちのおかずは、みいんな、
母(かあ)さまがおつくりなったもの。

私は好きになりたいな、
誰(だれ)でもかれでもみいんな。

I want to learn to like Everybody and Everything

I want to learn to like,
    Anything and everything.

Leeks, tomatoes, fish and all,
    I want to learn to like everything.

'Cause all the meals at home,
    My mother has specially made.

I want to learn to like,
    Anybody and everybody.

Even doctors, and crows,
    I want to learn to like, everybody and everything.

'Cause everybody and everything in this world,
    God has specially made.

お医者さんでも、烏でも、
残らず好きになりたいな。

世界のものはみィんな、
神さまがおつくりなったもの。

あるとき

お家(うち)のみえる角(かど)へ来(き)て、
おもい出したの、あのことを。
私(わたし)はもっと、ながいこと、
すねていなけりゃいけないの。
だって、かあさんはいったのよ、
「晩(ばん)までそうしておいで」って。
だのに、みんなが呼(よ)びにきて、
わすれて飛(と)んで出ちゃったの。

Once

Having come to the corner,
where I can see my house,
Now I remember that.

I should have stayed sulking,
For much longer.

'Cause my mother had said,
"Go on, stay like that until evening."

Despite this, when everyone called for me,
I forgot all about it and flew outside.

Now I feel awkward somehow,
But maybe it's alright,
'Cause my mother will surely prefer me,
In a good mood, after all.

なんだかきまりが悪いけど、
でもいいわ、
ほんとはきげんのいいほうが、
きっと、母さんは好きだから。

こころ

お母さまは
大人で大きいけれど。
お母さまの
おこころはちいさい。

だって、お母さまはいいました、
ちいさい私でいっぱいだって。

私は子供で
ちいさいけれど、
ちいさい私の
こころは大きい。

Hearts

Even though my mother
　Is big and grownup,
My mother's heart
　Must be small.

'Cause, my mother said,
　It's been all filled up with little me.

But, even though I am little
　And just a child,
My heart
　Must be big.

'Cause, my heart
　Can hold my big mother
And still have room for lots more.

だって、大きいお母さまで、
まだいっぱいにならないで、
いろんな事をおもうから。

口真似
——父さんのない子の唄——

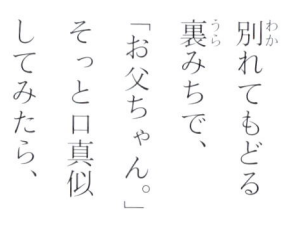

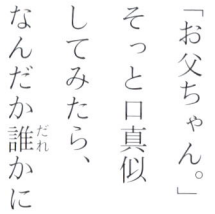

「お父ちゃん、
おしえてよう。」
あの子は甘えて
いっていた。

別れてもどる
裏みちで、
「お父ちゃん。」
そっと口真似
してみたら、
なんだか誰かに

Mimic
— A song of a fatherless child —

はずかしい。
生垣の しろい木槿が 笑うよう。

"Daddy,
　Come on, tell me, please."
The child said
In a begging manner.

　　　　After leaving them
　　　　On my way home in a back lane,
　　　　I now try to softly mimic,
　　　　"Daddy, please."
　　　　Yet somehow I feel shy
　　　　Although no one sees me.

A white 'mukuge' in the hedge
Seems to be laughing.

　　　　　　　　*mukuge = hibiscus syriacus

さびしいとき

私(わたし)がさびしいときに、
よその人は知(し)らないの。

私がさびしいときに、
お友(とも)だちは笑(わら)うの。

私がさびしいときに、
お母(かあ)さんはやさしいの。

私がさびしいときに、
仏(ほとけ)さまはさびしいの。

When I'm Lonely

When I'm lonely,
   Nobody else can tell.

When I'm lonely,
   My friends laugh.

When I'm lonely,
   My mother is kind.

When I'm lonely,
   Buddha is also lonely.

闇夜の星

闇夜に迷子の
星ひとつ。
あの子は
女の子でしょうか。
私のように
ひとりぼっちの、
あの子は
女の子でしょうか。

A Star in the Dark

In a moonless night
    A missing star is loosing it's way.
Is that a girl ?
    I wonder.

All alone like me ?
    Is that missing star,
A girl like me ?
    I wonder.

葉っぱの赤ちゃん

「ねんねなさい」は
月の役。
そっと光りを着せかけて、
だまってうたうねんね唄。

「起っきなさい」は
風の役。
東の空のしらむころ、
ゆすっておめめさませる。

昼のお守りは
小鳥たち。

みんなで唄をうたったり、
枝にかくれて、また出たり。

ちいさな
葉っぱの赤ちゃんは、
おっぱいのんでねんねして、
ねんねした間にふとります。

Tiny Baby Leaves

"Nighty night" is the role of the moon to play.
When it's light gently covers the tiny baby leaves,
It sings them lullabys in silence.

"Rise and shine" is the role of the wind to play.
When the sky in the east begins to whiten,
It shakes them till they wake up.

During the daytime the songbirds are their nursemaids.
They sometimes sing together,
        sometimes hide up on a branch,
And then show up again.

Those tiny baby leaves,
        suck their mother's milk and sleep,
And they grow big while falling asleep.

お花だったら

もしも私がお花なら、
とてもいい子になれるだろ。
ものが言えなきゃ、あるけなきゃ、
なんでおいたをするものか。
だけど、誰かがやって来て、
いやな花だといったなら、
すぐに怒ってしぼむだろ。

もしもお花になったって、
やっぱしいい子にゃなれまいな、
お花のようにはなれまいな。

If I Were a Flower

If I were a flower,
I would be a very good girl.

If you couldn't talk nor walk,
How could you play tricks, could you?

But, if someone came by and said,
　I hate you,
I would right away get angry
　And fade away.

So, even if I were a flower,
I would never be a good girl,
I would never ever be like a flower.

木

お花が散って
実(み)が熟(う)れて、
その実が落(お)ちて
葉(は)が落ちて
それから芽(め)が出て
花が咲(さ)く。
そうして何(なん)べん
まわったら、

A Tree

Flowers fall
Fruit ripens,

The fruit drops
Leaves fall,

Then, buds come out
And flowers bloom.

And so I wonder
How many times
This will go round,
Until this tree completes its task.

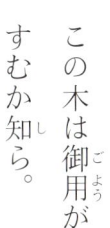

この木は御用がすむか知ら。

花のたましい

散ったお花のたましいは、
み仏（ほとけ）さまの花ぞのに、
ひとつ残（のこ）らずうまれるの。

だって、お花はやさしくて、
おてんとさまが呼（よ）ぶときに、
ぱっとひらいて、ほほえんで、
蝶々（ちょうちょう）にあまい蜜（みつ）をやり、
人にゃ匂（にお）いをみなくれて、
風（かぜ）がおいでとよぶときに、
やはりすなおについてゆき、

A Flower's Soul

The soul of a fallen flower,
Will be reborn in Buddha's flower garden,
With no exceptions.

Flowers are gentle and kind,
When the sun calls them,
They burst open and smile,
They give their sweet nectar to the butterflies,
And offer all their fragrance to people,

When the wind calls them to come,
They also follow obediently,

And they even allow their fallen petals,
To be used as food when children play house.

蓮と鶏

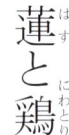

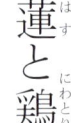

泥のなかから
蓮が咲く。

Lotus and Hens

Out of the mud
The lotus blooms.

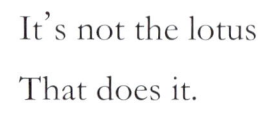

It's not the lotus
That does it.

Out of the egg
The chick comes.

It's not the chick
That does it.

This is what
I've realized.

But, it's not me
That does it.

それをするのは
蓮じゃない。

卵のなかから
鶏が出る。

それをするのは
鶏じゃない。

それに私は
気がついた。

それも私の
せいじゃない。

蜂と神さま

蜂はお花のなかに、
お花はお庭のなかに、
お庭は土塀のなかに、
土塀は町のなかに、
町は日本のなかに、
日本は世界のなかに、
世界は神さまのなかに。

そうして、そうして、神さまは、
小ちゃな蜂のなかに。

God and a Bee

A bee is inside a flower,
A flower is inside a garden,
A garden is inside a clay fence,
A clay fence is inside a town,
A town is inside Japan,
Japan is inside the world,
The world is inside of God.

And so, and so, God,
Is inside a little bee.

繭と墓

蚕(かいこ)は繭(まゆ)に
はいります、
きゅうくつそうな
あの繭(まゆ)に。

けれど蚕(かいこ)は
うれしかろ、
蝶々(ちょうちょう)になって
飛(と)べるのよ。

人(ひと)はお墓(はか)へ
はいります、
暗(くら)いさみしい
あの墓(はか)へ。

Cocoons and Graves

Silkworms

    Enter cocoons,

Tight looking

    Cocoons they are.

But silkworms

    Must be happy,

For they will become butterflies

    And fly.

People

    Enter graves,

Dark lonely

    Graves they are.

And if they are good

    They will grow wings,

And fly

    As angels.

そしていい子は
翅が生え、
天使になって
飛べるのよ。

明(あか)るい方(ほう)へ

明るい方へ
明るい方へ。
一つの葉(は)でも
陽(ひ)の洩(も)るとこへ。
籔(やぶ)かげの草(くさ)は。

明るい方へ
明るい方へ。
翅(はね)は焦(こ)げよと
灯(ひ)のあるとこへ。
夜(よる)飛(と)ぶ虫は。

明るい方へ
明るい方へ。
一分(いちぶ)もひろく
日の射(さ)すとこへ。
都会(まち)に住む子等(こら)は。

Towards the Light

Towards the light, towards the light.
Towards the place where the sun breaks through.
Even under the bushes
On a leaf of the grasses.

Towards the light, towards the light.
Towards the place where the light is on
Even the wings of the bugs be burned.
On the flying bugs in the night.

Towards the light, towards the light.
Towards the place where the sun beams down
Even a bit, the wider the better.
On the kids living in the city.

土

こっつん こっつん
打(ぶ)たれる土は
よい畠(はたけ)になって
よい麦(むぎう)生むよ。

朝(あさ)から晩(ばん)まで
踏(ふ)まれる土は
よい路(みち)になって
車(くるま)を通(とお)すよ。

打たれぬ土は

The Ground

Pound pound
The pounded ground
Will become a good field
And bear good barley.

The trodden ground
From morning till night
Will become a good road
For cars to pass along.

But what about the unpounded
And untrodden ground
Is this ground useless?

No no
It will be a good home
For the unknown wild grass.

草原(そうげん)

露(つゆ)の草原
はだしでゆけば、
足があおあお染(そ)まるよな。
草(くさ)のにおいもうつるよな。

草になるまで
あるいてゆけば、
私(わたし)のおかおはうつくしい、
お花になって、咲(さ)くだろう。

Grass

When I walk barefoot
　On a field of dewy grass,
It feels like my feet get greener and greener.
It also feels like the grassy smell gets into them.

If I keep on walking
　Until I become the grass,
My face will become a beautiful flower,
And bloom.

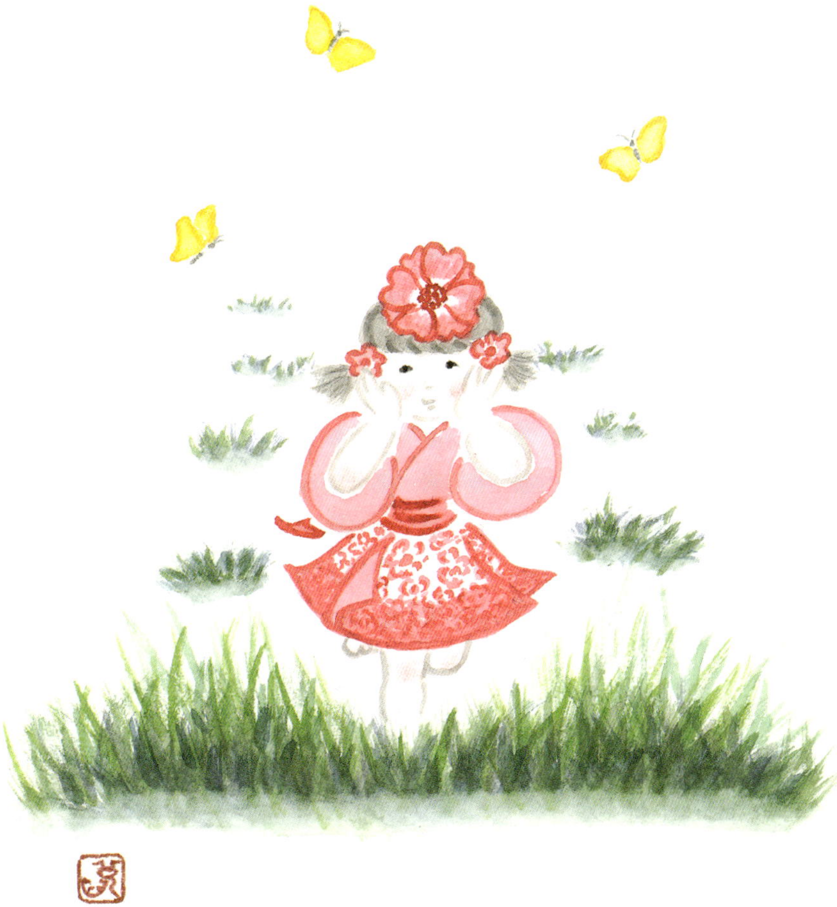

露（つゆ）

誰（だれ）にもいわずにおきましょう。
朝（あさ）のお庭（にわ）のすみっこで、
花（はな）がほろりと泣（な）いたこと。

もしも噂（うわさ）がひろがって
蜂（はち）のお耳（みみ）へはいったら、
わるいことでもしたように、
蜜（みつ）をかえしに行（ゆ）くでしょう。

The Dewdrop

Well, I won't tell it to anyone.

That a flower was moved to tears in silence,
In a corner of the garden this morning.

If words get around
And the honeybee hears it,

It will go and put the nectar back,
As if it had done something wrong.

ばあやのお話

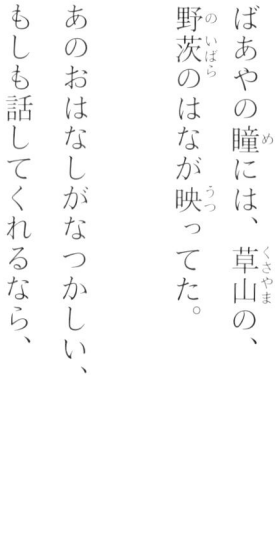

ばあやはあれきり話さない、
あのおはなしは、好きだのに。

「もうきいたよ」といったとき、
ずいぶんさびしい顔してた。

ばあやの瞳には、草山の、
野茨のはなが映ってた。

あのおはなしがなつかしい、
もしも話してくれるなら、

Nanny's Story

Nanny won't tell me that story anymore,
    Even though I really liked it.

When I told her "I've heard this before."
    Her face turned very sad.

I saw wild roses on a grassy hill,
    Reflected in nanny's eyes.

I miss that story now,
If she would only tell it to me again,
    I promise I'd listen to it,
    For five or even ten times,
    Silent and well-behaved.

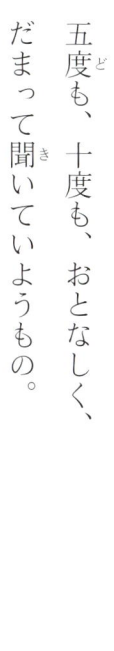

五度（ど）も、十度も、おとなしく、
だまって聞（き）いていようもの。

ふうせん

ふうせん持った子が
そばにいて、
私が持ってるようでした。

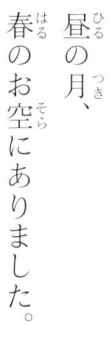

ぴい、とどこぞで
笛がなる、
まつりのあとの裏どおり、

あかいふうせん、
昼の月、
春のお空にありました。

ふうせん持った子が
行っちゃって、
すこしさみしくなりました。

A Balloon

A child holding a balloon was next to me,
Somehow I felt like I was holding it too.

Somewhere sound of piping music was heard,
After the festival on the back street,

A red balloon and a moon at noon,
Both are up in the spring sky.

Somewhere the child holding the balloon has gone,
Somehow I felt a bit lonely too.

極楽寺(ごくらくじ)

極楽寺のさくらは八重(やえ)ざくら、
八重ざくら、
使(つか)いにゆくとき見(み)て来(き)たよ。
横町(よこちょう)の四(よ)つ角(かど)まがるとき(とき)、
まがる時、
よこ目でちらりと見て来たよ。
極楽寺のさくらは土ざくら、
土ざくら、
土の上ばかりに咲(さ)いてたよ。

Gokurakuji Temple
(The 7th Heaven Temple)

The cherry blossoms at the Gokurakuji Temple

Are double, are double petalled,

While I was on an errand

I saw them in bloom.

When I turned at the byways,

When I turned at the four corners,

I took a glance at them.

The other cherry blossoms at the Gokurakuji Temple

Are blooming on the ground,

They are the ground cherry blossom,

Flowering only on the ground.

Carrying my lunchbox of wakame (seeweed) rice balls

With me, with me,

I went to see them all

And I saw them all.

若布結飯のお弁当で、
お弁当で、
さくら見に行って見てきたよ。

八百屋のお鳩

おや鳩子ばと
お鳩が三羽
八百屋の軒で
クックと啼いた。

茄子はむらさき
キャベツはみどり
いちごの赤も
つやつやぬれて。

The Doves at the Green Grocer's

Papa, mama and their baby dove

A family of three doves

On the green grocer's eaves.
    Cooed.

Eggplants are purple

Cabbages are green

And the strawberry's red color

Looks glossy wet.

Well, well, well, what shall I buy?

The white doves

On the green grocer's eaves
    Cooed.

祇園社

はらはら
松の葉が落ちる、
お宮の秋は
さみしいな。

のぞきの唄よ
瓦斯の灯よ、
赤い帯した
肉桂よ。

いまは
こわれた氷屋に、
さらさら
秋風ふくばかり。

Gion Shrine

By ones and by twos
The pine needles are fluttering down,
Autumn in the Gion Shrine is lonesome.

Oh, a song of a peep show box
Oh, a light of a gas lamp,
Oh, a bundle of red bonded cinnamons.

Through the now deserted ice house,
Only the autumn wind is murmuring.

積った雪

上の雪
さむかろな。
つめたい月がさしていて。

下の雪
重(おも)かろな。
何百人ものせていて。

中の雪
さみしかろな。
空も地面(じべた)もみえないで。

A Pile of Snow

The snow on the top

    Must feel cold.

Lit by the icy cold moonlight.

The snow at the bottom

    Must feel burdened.

Bearing the weight of hundreds of people.

The snow in the middle

    Must feel lonely.

It can see neither sky nor ground.

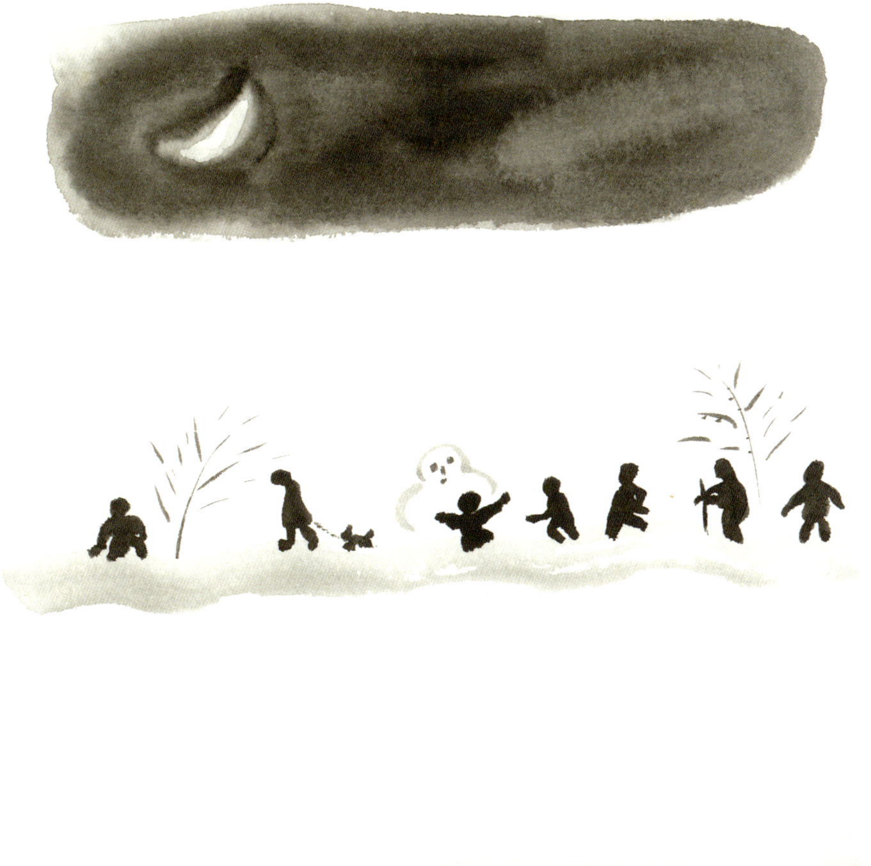

硝子のなか

おもての雪が見えるので、
ひらひらお花のようなので、
明り障子の絵硝子を、
お炬燵にあたって見ていたら、
うらの木小屋へ木をとりに、
雪ふるなかを歩いてく、
お祖母さまのうしろかげ、
ちらちら映って、消えました。

Through the Glass

I can see the snow outside,
Fluttering like flowers,
While I look through the patterned 'akari-shoji' glass,
I warm myself under the 'kotatsu' table,

Walking through the snow,
To fetch some wood from the woodshed at the back,
Grandma has her figure reflected,
Momentarily on the glass, then it fades away.

*akari-shoji = sliding paper screen door with a glass pane in the center to allow in extra light.

*kotatsu = a foot warmer covered with a quilt.

大漁

朝焼小焼だ
大漁だ
大羽鰮の
大漁だ。

浜は祭りの
ようだけど
海のなかでは
何万の
鰮のとむらい
するだろう。

A Big Catch

Morning glow, sunrise glow
   A big catch
   A big catch of Ōba sardines.

On the beach
   People may have a feast
But meanwhile
   Under the ocean
Thousands of sardines
   Will mourn for the dead.

*ōba sardine = a kind of big sardine

お魚

海の魚はかわいそう。

お米は人につくられる、
牛は牧場で飼われてる、
鯉もお池で麩を貰う。

けれども海のお魚は
なんにも世話にならないし
いたずら一つしないのに
こうして私に食べられる。

ほんとに魚はかわいそう。

Fish

I feel sorry for the fish in the sea.

    The rice in the field is cultivated by man,
    The cows in the pasture are raised by man,
    The carp in the pond too are fed by man.

But the fish in the sea
    Are under the care of nobody at all
    And even though they never cause any trouble
    They're eaten by me just like this.

I really feel sorry for the fish.

帆（ほ）

港（みなと）に着（つ）いた舟（ふね）の帆（ほ）は、
みんな古（ふる）びて黒（くろ）いのに、
はるかの沖（おき）をゆく舟は、
光りかがやく白い帆ばかり。

はるかの沖の、あの舟は、
いつも、港へつかないで、
海（うみ）とお空のさかいめばかり、
はるかに遠（とお）く行くんだよ。

かがやきながら、行くんだよ。

Sails

All the sails of the ships docked at port,
   Look old and grey,
Yet all the ships that sail far out to sea,
   Have sails sparkling white.

But these ships, far out to sea,
   Will never ever reach a port,
They are always sailing,
   On the horizon of sea and sky,
Going farther away.

Sparkling away.

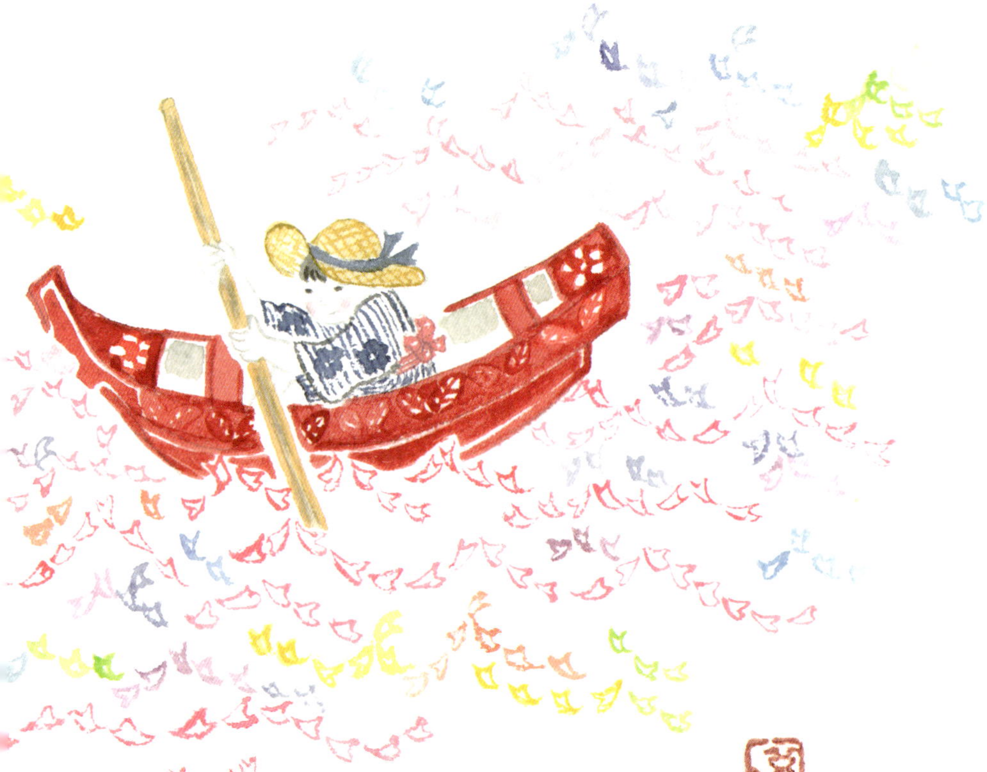

みんなちがって、
みんないい。

We're all different,
　　　　And all wonderful.

あとがき

一九三〇年、二十六歳という若さで散ってしまった女流詩人、金子みすゞ。

その詩に深く感動した私は絵を描き、さらに、この素晴らしい詩人の作品を世界中の人々に知っていただきたいとの思いから、みすゞの詩を英訳しました。

みすゞの詩の中に溢れる宇宙観的普遍性、温かく繊細な感性の世界観が、一人でも多くの方々に伝わりましたら、大いなる喜びです。

訳にあたっては、ジュリー・ロジャーズさんとエリザベス・レイジェックさんのご協力を得ましたこと、そして又、出版に際しましては、藤原書店の藤原良雄社長、編集者の山﨑優子氏にお世話になりましたことを感謝します。尚、みすゞの詩は『金子みすゞ全集』全三巻（JULA出版局、一九九三）から依拠しました。最後に、みすゞの遺稿を探し出し出版された児童文学者の矢崎節夫氏に深く敬意を表します。

　　　　　　よしだみどり

Postscript

Misuzu Kaneko, a gifted young poetess who died in 1930 at the age of 26, has deeply impressed me with her profound love, penetrating insight and subtle observations of the world in which she lived. Because of these facts I have decided to convey her philosophy and sentiment by publishing my illustrations and translations of some of her poems.

I sincerely hope to have as many readers as possible to learn about her message of universal truth.

I am very grateful to Ms. Julie Rogers and Dr. Elizabeth M. Rajec for their help translating Misuzu Kaneko's poems. My hearty appreciation also goes to the President of Fujiwara Shoten Publishing Co., Mr. Yoshio Fujiwara and to the Editor Ms. Yuko Yamazaki.

The poems of Misuzu are selected from "The Complete Works (the three volumes) of Kaneko Misuzu" (JULA Syuppankyoku, 1993).
In addition, I would express my gratitude to Mr. Setsuo Yazaki, a literary specialist of children's literature who discovered and published the manuscripts left by the late Misuzu Kaneko.

Midori Yoshida

金子みすゞ（かねこ・みすず）

1903（明治36）年、山口県大津郡仙崎村（現在の長門市仙崎）に生まれる。本名、金子テル。大津高等女学校を卒業。1920年代半ば（大正末期〜昭和初期）、『童話』『婦人倶楽部』等にすぐれた詩作品を発表し、西條八十に「若き童謡詩人の巨星」とまで称賛されながら、1930（昭和5）年、自ら命を絶った（享年満26歳）。

没後、その作品は埋もれ、幻の童謡詩人として語り継がれるばかりになったが、近年、512編の詩を収めた遺稿集が出版され、「私と小鳥と鈴と」など多くの人々に口ずさまれる存在として甦った。

Misuzu Kaneko

Born in 1903 in Senzaki (presently Nagato City), Yamaguchi Prefecture. She wrote poems for children and earned the praise of Yaso Saijo, who called her "The Star of Poets for Children". She was also admitted to be a member of "The Nursery Rhymes Poets Society".

Since she committed suicide at the age of 26, after her death, most of her writings were lost and her name was passed to later generations as merely a phantom of children's poetess.

In recent years, her 512 poems were published and these beautiful poems have found their way into people's heart.

よしだ みどり

作家。画家。日本テレビ幼児教育番組「ロンパールーム」司会をつとめた（1969〜4年間）。キングレコードよりＬＰヒット賞（「ロンパールーム」歌唱・よしだみどり）受賞。スティーヴンスンの生涯を描いた『物語る人』（毎日新聞社）で平成12年度「日本文芸大賞　伝記翻訳新人賞」受賞。

著書に『知られざる「吉田松陰伝」──『宝島』のスティーヴンスンがなぜ？』（祥伝社）他。訳書に『びんの悪魔』（福音館書店）『セレンディピティ物語』（藤原書店）。画に『金子みすゞ花の詩集』『花のたましひ』（JULA出版局）他。編書に『竹内浩三楽書き詩集』『竹内浩三集』（藤原書店）他。

Midori Yoshida

Author and artist, worked for the educational program "Romper Room" as the teacher on TV. She received "The Best Selling Disc of The Year Award" from the King Record Co., Ltd. She is also the recipient of "The Newcomer Award of Biography and Translation of Poetry" for her book "Teller of Tales (Monogataruhito)" from the Society of Literary Arts of Japan.

She arranged many exhibitions of her paintings and illustrations in Japan by the title "The World of Kaneko Misuzu's Poetry".

She is the translator of "The Child Garden of Verses" and "The Bottle Imp" by R. L. Stevenson.

―― 付録ＣＤ ――

1　　　　　（歌）私と小鳥と鈴と
2〜8　　　（朗読）星とたんぽぽ〜犬
9　　　　　（歌）みんなを好きに
10〜18　　（朗読）女の子〜さびしいとき
19　　　　（歌）星とたんぽぽ
20〜29　　（朗読）闇夜の星〜土
30　　　　（歌）わらい
31〜42　　（朗読）草原〜帆
43　　　　（歌）大漁
44〜49　　（英語）Stars and a Dandelion 〜 Mystery
50　　　　（歌）犬
51〜57　　（英語）The Dog 〜 Once
58　　　　（歌）こころ
59〜72　　（英語）Hearts 〜 Grass
73　　　　（歌）露
74〜79　　（英語）The Dewdrop 〜 Gion Shrine
80　　　　（歌）積った雪
81〜85　　（英語）A Pile of Snow 〜 Sails
86　　　　（歌）こだまでしょうか

＊ＣＤの朗読は、本書の順番で収録されています。
＊金子みすゞの詩は『金子みすゞ全集』より。
　収録に際し旧漢字・旧かなづかいは新漢字・新かなづかいに改めました。

金子みすゞ　心の詩集　The Poetry of Misuzu
特別付録 CD〔歌・朗読〕

2012年3月20日　初版第1刷発行©

編　者　よしだみどり
発行者　藤原良雄
発行所　株式会社　藤原書店
〒162-0041　東京都新宿区早稲田鶴巻町523
電　話　03（5272）0301
FAX　03（5272）0450
振　替　00160‐4‐17013
info@fujiwara-shoten.co.jp

印刷・製本　中央精版印刷

落丁本・乱丁本はお取替えいたします　　Printed in Japan
定価はカバーに表示してあります　　ISBN978-4-89434-846-2

⦿「セレンディピティ」の語源の物語

セレンディピティ物語
〔幸せを招ぶ三人の王子〕

E・J・ホッジス
よしだみどり訳・画

父が息子に与える難問、まいごのラクダ、女王のなぞなぞ、摩訶不思議な怪物たち——ノーベル賞受賞者など多くの科学者、芸術家たちが好んで使う言葉「セレンディピティ」の語源となった三人の王子の冒険物語。

A5上製　二四〇頁　二四〇〇円
（二〇〇六年四月刊）
◇978-4-89434-512-6

THE THREE PRINCES OF SERENDIP
Elizabeth Jamison HODGES

⊙「マンガのきらいなヤツは入るべからず」

竹内浩三楽書き詩集 まんがのよろづや

よしだみどり編
[絵・詩]竹内浩三
[色・構成]よしだみどり

一九四五年、比島にて二十三歳で戦死した「天性の詩人」竹内浩三。そのみずみずしい感性で自作の回覧雑誌などに描いた、十五〜二十二歳の「まんが」や詩をオールカラーで再構成。浩三の詩／絵／マンガが、初めて一緒に楽しめる！

A5上製　七二頁［オールカラー］一八〇〇円
（二〇〇五年七月刊）
◇978-4-89434-465-5

◉詩と自筆の絵で立体的に構成

竹内浩三集

竹内浩三・文と絵
よしだみどり編

泣き虫で笑い上戸、淋しがりやでお姉さんっ子、「よくふられる代わりによくホレる」……天賦のユーモアに溢れながら、人間の暗い内実を鋭く抉る言葉。しかし底抜けの明るさで笑い飛ばすコーゾー少年の青春。自ら描いたユニークなマンガとの絶妙な取り合わせに、涙と笑いが止まらない!

B6変上製 二七二頁 二三〇〇円
(二〇〇六年一〇月刊)
◇ 978-4-89434-528-7

◉活字／写真版の完全版

竹内浩三全作品集（全一巻）
日本が見えない

小林察編
［推薦］吉増剛造

太平洋戦争のさ中にあって、時代の不安を率直に綴り、戦後の高度成長から今日の日本の腐敗を見抜いた詩人、「骨のうたう」の竹内浩三の全作品を、活字と写真版で収めた完全版。新発見の詩二篇と日記も収録。「本当に生きた弾みのある声」（吉増剛造氏）。

菊大上製貼函入　七三六頁［口絵一二四頁］八八〇〇円
（二〇〇一年一一月刊）
◇ 978-4-89434-261-3

◉三八億年の生命の歴史がミュージカルに

いのち愛づる姫
[ものみな一つの細胞から]

中村桂子・山崎陽子作
堀文子画

全ての生き物をゲノムから読み解く「生命誌」を提唱した生物学者、中村桂子。ピアノ一台で夢の舞台を演出する"朗読ミュージカル"を創りあげた童話作家、山崎陽子。いのちの気配を写し続けてきた画家、堀文子。各分野で第一線の三人が描きだす、いのちのハーモニー。

B5変上製　八〇頁［カラー六四頁］　一八〇〇円
（二〇〇七年四月刊）
◇ 978-4-89434-565-2

◉沖縄から日本をひらくために

真振 MABUI

海勢頭豊

写真＝市毛實

沖縄に踏みとどまり魂（ＭＡＢＵＩ）を生きる姿が、本島や本土の多くの人々に深い感銘を与えてきた伝説のミュージシャン、初の半生の物語。喪われた日本人の心の源流である沖縄の、最も深い精神世界を語り下ろす。

Ｂ５変並製　一七六頁　二八〇〇円
＊ＣＤ付「月桃」「喜瀬武原」
（二〇〇三年六月刊）
◇978-4-89434-344-3

◉ いのちと自然にみちたくらしの美しさ

石牟礼道子 詩文コレクション（全7巻）

1 猫　[解説]町田康
2 花　[解説]河瀨直美
3 渚　[解説]吉増剛造
4 色　[解説]伊藤比呂美
5 音　[解説]大倉正之助
6 父　[解説]小池昌代
7 母　[解説]米良美一

（題字）石牟礼道子　（画）よしだみどり　（装丁）作間順子
B6変上製　各巻一九二〜二三二頁　各二三〇〇円
各巻著者あとがき／解説／しおり付